Thank you, dear apple trees, for your
nourishment, inspiration, and beauty—D.C.
To Clément, with all my love—G.G

Brimming with creative inspiration, how-to projects, and useful information to enrich your everyday life, Quarto Knows is a favourite destination for those pursuing their interests and passions. Visit our site and dig deeper with our books into your area of interest: Quarto Creates, Quarto Cooks, Quarto Homes, Quarto Lives, Quarto Drives, Quarto Explores, Quarto Gifts, or Quarto Kids.

Text © 2019 Dawn Casey. Illustrations © 2019 Genevieve Godbout.
First published in 2019 by Frances Lincoln Children's Books,
an imprint of The Quarto Group,
400 First Avenue North, Suite 400, Minneapolis, MN 55401, USA.
T (612) 344-8100 F (612) 344-8692 www.QuartoKnows.com
The right of Dawn Casey to be identified as the author and
Genevieve Godbout to be identified as the illustrator of this work
has been asserted by them in accordance with the Copyright,
Designs and Patents Act, 1988 (United Kingdom).

A catalogue record for this book is available
from the British Library.
ISBN 978-1-78603-215-7
The illustrations were created with soft pastels and colored pencil
Set in Memphis
Published and edited by Katie Cotton
Designed by Karissa Santos
Production by Nicolas Zeifman

Manufactured in the United States of America CG112019
3 5 7 9 8 6 4 2

Apple Cake

Frances Lincoln
Children's Books

Thank you, hedge,
thank you, tree.

Thank you, flower,
thank you, bee.

Thank you, rain,
thank you, sun.

Thank you, farmers,
every one.

Thank you, cows,
thank you, hens.

Thank you, family,
thank you, friends.

Thank you earth
beneath our feet.

Thank you for
the food we eat.

Hedge and tree,
flower, bee,
cows and hens,
family, friends,
earth and water,
fire and air,

thank you for
the gifts you
share.

Thank you for the
food we make.
Thank you all for
apple cake.

Recipe for Apple Cake

Ingredients:
½ cup apples
4 eggs
½ cup honey
½ cup butter, melted (or coconut oil, as a dairy-free alternative)
3 cups nuts, ground to make flour (you can use hazelnuts, or almond flour, or a mixture of both)
½ teaspoon baking soda

Instructions:
1. Preheat the oven to 325°F.
2. Line a baking dish with parchment paper.
3. Prepare the apples: Peel the apples with a vegetable peeler. (See if you can peel the skin in one curly coil—then you can eat it!) Cut the apples into pieces.
4. Here is a safe way for young children to cut apples all on their own:
- On a cutting board, a grown-up cuts across the center of the apple.
- Appreciate the star hidden within.
- Put the halves cut side down onto the board.

- Children can use a short knife, with a not-too-sharp blade, to cut down through the apple, as if cutting slices of cake.
- Children can lay each slice down flat on the cutting board to cut out the piece of core visible, and then cut the apple chunk into pieces.

5. Measure half a cup full of apple pieces.
6. In one bowl, mix together the ground nut flour and the baking soda.
7. In another bowl, whisk together the eggs, honey, and butter. Then mix in the apple pieces.
8. Mix everything together, put the mixture in the dish, and bake the cake in the oven for 40 minutes.
9. Serve warm with fresh cream.

For special occasions, a topping and glaze can be added.

Topping:
1. Prepare 3 apples: Cut the apples in half, remove the cores, and cut the apple pieces into thin slices.
2. Prepare two pots of water; one of boiling water, one of ice-cold water.
3. Blanch the apple slices in the boiling water for one minute, to soften.
4. Transfer the apple slices into the ice-water, to stop the cooking process.
5. Place the apple slices on a paper towel to dry off any water.
6. Arrange the apple slices on top of the cooled cake: start from the outer edge, working toward the center, to form a circular pattern.

Glaze:
1. Melt 2 tbsp of runny honey with 1 tbsp butter (or coconut oil).
2. Bring to the boil, stirring.
3. Boil for one minute, stirring.
4. Leave to cool for a few minutes.
5. Spoon over the cake, allowing the glaze to drizzle over the sides.
6. Enjoy your apple cake warm with cream.